J EASY MARZOLLO
Marzollo, Jean.
Soccer cousins

Withdrawn/ABCI

D0475240

RIO GRANDE VALLEY
LIBRARY SYSTEM (F)

A NOTE TO PARENTS

Reading Aloud with Your Child
Research shows that reading books aloud is the single most valuable support parents can provide in helping children learn to read.
- Be a ham! The more enthusiasm you display, the more your child will enjoy the book.
- Run your finger underneath the words as you read to signal that the print carries the story.
- Leave time for examining the illustrations more closely; encourage your child to find things in the pictures.
- Invite your youngster to join in whenever there's a repeated phrase in the text.
- Link up events in the book with similar events in your child's life.
- If your child asks a question, stop and answer it. The book can be a means to learning more about your child's thoughts.

Listening to Your Child Read Aloud
The support of your attention and praise is absolutely crucial to your child's continuing efforts to learn to read.
- If your child is learning to read and asks for a word, give it immediately so that the meaning of the story is not interrupted. DO NOT ask your child to sound out the word.
- On the other hand, if your child initiates the act of sounding out, don't intervene.
- If your child is reading along and makes what is called a miscue, listen for the sense of the miscue. If the word "road" is substituted for the word "street," for instance, no meaning is lost. Don't stop the reading for a correction.
- If the miscue makes no sense (for example, "horse" for "house"), ask your child to reread the sentence because you're not sure you understand what's just been read.
- Above all else, enjoy your child's growing command of print and make sure you give lots of praise. *You are your child's first teacher — and the most important one. Praise from you is critical for further risk-taking and learning.*

— Priscilla Lynch
Ph.D. New York University
Educational Consultant

*This book is dedicated with affection
and appreciation to Hugo Mendez, his family, two
teachers — Manuel Narváez Acevedo and Zeferino
Olea Vázquez — and their students at Escuela Primaria
Urbana General Presidente "Lázaro Cárdenas"
in Huajuapan de León, Oaxaca, México
— J.M. and I.T.*

No part of this publication may be reproduced, or stored in a retrieval system, or transmitted in any form or by any means, electronic, mechanical, photocopying, recording, or otherwise, without written permission of the publisher. For information regarding permission, write to Scholastic Inc., Attention: Permissions Department, 555 Broadway, New York, NY 10012.

Text copyright © 1997 by Jean Marzollo.
Illustrations copyright © 1997 by Irene Trivas.
All rights reserved. Published by Scholastic Inc.
HELLO READER! and CARTWHEEL BOOKS and associated logos
are trademarks and/or registered trademarks of Scholastic Inc.

Library of Congress Cataloging-in-Publication Data
Marzollo, Jean.
Soccer cousins / by Jean Marzollo ; illustrated by Irene Trivas.
p.   cm.— (Hello reader! Level 4)
"Cartwheel Books."
Summary: When David visits his cousin in Mexico, he not only celebrates the Day of the Dead but he also plays a big part in Miguel's soccer tournament.
ISBN 0-590-74254-X
[1. Soccer — Fiction. 2. Cousins — Fiction. 3. All Souls' Day — Mexico — Fiction. 4. Grandfathers — Fiction. 5. Mexico — Fiction.]
I. Trivas, Irene, ill. II. Title. III. Series.
PZ7.M3688Sno   1997
[Fic] — DC20
96-7292
CIP
AC

10 9 8 7 6 5 4 3 2 1   7 8 9/9 0/0 01 02
Printed in the U.S.A.   24
First printing, October 1997

Withdrawn/ABCL

Soccer Cousins

by Jean Marzollo
Illustrated by Irene Trivas

Hello Reader!—Level 4

RIO GRANDE VALLEY
LIBRARY SYSTEM

SCHOLASTIC INC.
Cartwheel ·B·O·O·K·S·®

New York Toronto London Auckland Sydney

The Day of the Dead
El Día de los Muertos *(el DEE-ah dey los MWER-tos)*

The Day of the Dead is a Mexican holiday that honors and celebrates relatives and friends who have died. Many people believe that during this joyful, spiritual, and beautiful holiday, the spirits of dead relatives and friends return to eat their favorite foods and to be with the people they loved.
The skulls and skeletons seen on the Day of the Dead are painted bright, friendly colors, conveying the belief that the spirit lives on after the body dies. Celebrated on All Saints' Day, November 1 and on All Souls' Day, November 2, the Day of the Dead combines pre-Hispanic beliefs with Spanish Roman Catholic traditions.

The last game was almost over. David's team was losing 2 – 1.

David was near the goal. The ball came right to him.

"Shoot, David!" shouted the coach.

But David was scared he would miss. So he didn't kick the ball.

David's team lost.

"You play well during practice," said his coach. "But during games you freeze. Next year I'm sure you'll play better."

David said nothing to his coach.

But to himself he said, "I will never *play* soccer again. From now on, I will only *watch* soccer games."

At home, the phone rang.

It was David's cousin Miguel! He called from Mexico. Miguel's soccer team was going to play in a tournament.

"Do you want to come to Mexico to watch us?" asked Miguel. "Papá is the coach."

David said, "Sure!"

But the tournament started October 30.

"That's the day before Halloween!" said David. "I have a new monster costume!"

"Bring it!" said Miguel. "You can wear it on the Day of the Dead."

David had heard about the Day of the Dead. It
was a wonderful holiday in Mexico. David's mother
had told him about it. She had grown up in Mexico.

"We decorate graves with flowers and candles,"
she said. "We have candy, music, and fireworks."

She thought David would have fun. She said he
could take a few days off from school.

"Aren't you coming, too?" asked David.

"This year we only have money for one ticket,"
she said. "You're old enough to fly alone now."

So David went to Mexico.

"Prepare for landing," said the pilot.

David looked out the window. Mexico City was huge!

"Your cousin's family will be meeting you," said the flight attendant. "Have a good time in Mexico!"

A nice woman checked David's passport. A man checked his suitcase. Then David walked through a big door and saw his cousin.

"¡Hola!" shouted Miguel.

"¡Hola!" shouted David. He gave Miguel a big hug. He also hugged Tía, his aunt, and Tío, his uncle.

"You brave boy," said Tío proudly. "You fly alone."

"Sí," said David. His mother had told him to try to speak Spanish.

David and his relatives rode a bus through Mexico City. Miguel talked about the tournament. His English was excellent because he learned to speak it in school.

"Tomorrow are the semifinals," he said. "We play los Pumas. Los Pumas means the Cougars. They stink. We can beat them. Papá says you can sit with us on the team bench."

"¡Bueno!" said David. The bench would be a good place to *watch* the game.

The bus was now on a winding road in the mountains. Tío spoke in Spanish to David. He spoke so fast! David didn't understand a word.

"He says your mama told him you are a good player," said Miguel.

"Gracias," said David. He didn't know how to tell Tío that he was never going to *play* soccer again.

Sí. Hola. Bueno. Gracias. They were the only
Spanish words David could remember.

David was hot and tired. He closed his eyes.
He slept all the way to Miguel's city.

The next day David awoke to the smell of chocolate. He and Miguel went to the kitchen.

"Do you eat chocolate for breakfast?" he asked.

"No, we eat tortillas," said Miguel. He smiled. "What you smell are the candies Abuelita is making for Abuelito."

Abuelita was their grandmother. Abuelito was their grandfather. He had been a famous soccer player when he was alive.

"Abuelito died last year," said David. "Why is she cooking for him?"

"We're getting ready for the Day of the Dead," said Miguel. "We will honor Abuelito. He loved chocolate! We will bring some to his grave so his spirit will visit us."

"Do you think his spirit will really come?" asked David.

"I hope so," said Miguel. "We need good luck for the final game!"

"What about the semifinal game today?" asked David.

"We don't need luck for that," said Miguel. "Los Pumas are terrible. Today's game will be easy."

But it wasn't easy. The game had no score until the end. Then one of the Eagles scored. It wasn't Miguel, but his team still won.

Miguel sat down next to David in disgust. David passed him an orange.

"I was awful," said Miguel. "I didn't score one goal."

David didn't say anything. He was glad that the Eagles won. But part of him was glad that Miguel hadn't scored. Maybe now Miguel would be afraid to play soccer, too.

Tío drew his team around him. He spoke rapidly. Miguel translated. "The good news is that we won. The bad news is that we are going to play los Tiburones in the finals. Los Tiburones means the Sharks. They are a great team."

The next morning Miguel woke David. "I had a nightmare about sharks," he said. "Please. Will you practice soccer with me?"

David almost said no. But he felt bad for his cousin. So he agreed to play. But not in a real game. Never, ever again.

David and Miguel set up a goal with boxes in the courtyard. They ran. They kicked. They scored. It was fun!

Tío came out and watched. He spoke in Spanish.

Miguel translated. "He says that you are a good player. If you lived here, you could play on our team."

No, thanks, thought David.

Abuelita came outside. "¡Vamos al mercado!" she said.

"We have to go to the market now," said Miguel.

The market was a big outdoor store. It was filled with food, flowers, candles, balloons, and candy.

Some of the candies were shaped like skulls. Others were shaped like skeletons.

"In Mexico we celebrate the dead," explained Miguel. David and Miguel each bought a candy skull.

Miguel bought himself a clown mask. Suddenly he looked scared. "Behind you!" he said. "The Sharks are coming!"

"What should we do?" asked David.

"Hide," said Miguel. He put on his mask. David hid behind some flowers.

The Sharks were talking about the Eagles. "They say we play like babies," whispered Miguel. "I can't believe it. For the first time, I'm afraid to play a soccer game."

You're starting to feel like me, thought David.

That afternoon the boys practiced again.
Again, David had fun! If only real games were
like practice.

The next morning the boys helped Abuelita make an altar for Abuelito. She hung flowers on the wall. David and Miguel added fruit, bread, candles, and candies.

Abuelita contributed a photograph of Abuelito. "What else would make him happy?" she asked.

"His trophies!" said Miguel.

Abuelita brought trophies and medals from a drawer. Miguel and David put them on the altar. The table was splendid.

"Please, Abuelito! Send your spirit to visit us," said Miguel. "We need you!"

The boys went with Tío to the cemetery. They painted Abuelito's grave blue and purple. Abuelita brought candles and flowers.

Finally, the grave was done. It was beautiful!

That night the whole family went to the cemetery. David wore his monster costume. Miguel wore a clown costume. Outside the cemetery, a band was playing cheerful music. People were selling food and balloons. David and Miguel ate tamales and drank cola.

Abuelito's grave was a peaceful place to be. The other graves were wonderful, too.

"Is he here?" David asked.

"Tomorrow," said Abuelita.

"And the fireworks?" asked David.

"Tomorrow," said Abuelita.

The next day David called his mother. "Mom," he said. "Everyone hopes Abuelito's spirit will come tonight. Do you think that's possible?"

"I don't know," she said. "But if he does, tell him I miss him. And tell Miguel good luck in the game!"

"My mom says good luck," David told Miguel.

"I need it," said Miguel. "I'm scared of those Sharks. What if Abuelito doesn't come? Maybe we need to add more decorations to the altar."

Miguel showed David how to fold paper and cut designs. They hung their pictures around the table.

Abuelita sprinkled fried chicken with lime juice.

"¡Abuelito!" shouted Miguel. "Do you smell that?
Is your spirit going to come and visit us tonight?"

The family carried Abuelito's favorite foods to his
grave: tortillas, chicken in lime juice, rice and beans,
tomatoes, and chocolate. Everything was delicious!

"Is Abuelito here?" asked David.

"I can't feel him," said Miguel. He looked a
little worried.

Music played. Fireworks exploded in the air.

"Wow!" said David.

But when the fireworks were over, Miguel still looked worried. He spoke in Spanish to Abuelita. Abuelita shook her head. She looked sad, too.

The day of the final game was here. At breakfast Tío said, "Don't think about Abuelito. Think about the game."

But just before they left the house, Abuelita took David aside. "Take this," she whispered. She gave David one of Abuelito's medals and a little candy. "Maybe he'll come to the game," she said.

"Sí," said David. He put the medal and candy in his pocket.

David sat on the bench and watched the game start. The crowd cheered.

Both teams were nervous. One of the Eagles hurt his knee. He couldn't play anymore. He sat down near David.

The game continued. The Sharks were very fast! They scored two goals.

Then another accident happened. An Eagle sprained his shoulder. He was taken out of the game.

Tío was very worried. At halftime, he said, "If we lose one more player, we'll have to quit. We won't have enough players to finish the game."

The game began again. And then, the worst happened. A third player on the Eagles was injured. He had to lie down.

The Eagles now had only ten players. They needed eleven. The two coaches and referees met in the middle of the field.

Everyone watched them.

All of a sudden, Tío pointed at David.

"No," whispered David. "Not me."

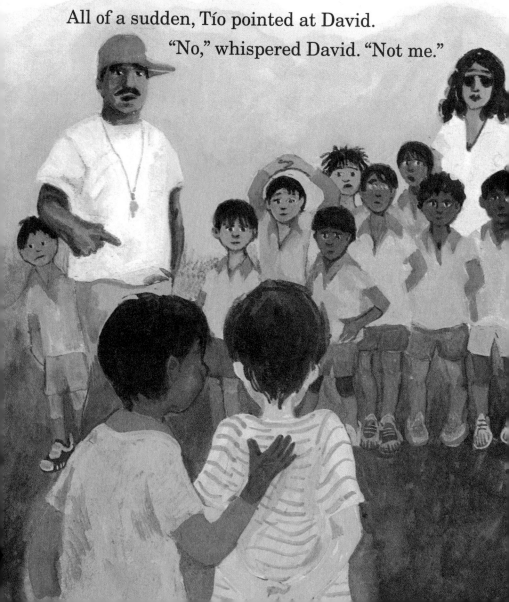

Then he imagined a voice behind him. "Sí," said the voice. It sounded just like his grandfather used to sound.

"No," whispered David.

"Sí," said the deep voice. The voice was cheerful and kind.

Tío spoke in Spanish to Miguel. Miguel spoke in English to David. "The other coach wants to keep playing. The referees said they will let you play. Will you play with us?"

David wanted to say no. But when he opened his mouth, he said, "Sí."

David put on a uniform, and the game started again. Miguel had the ball. He passed it to David. David wondered, *Do I dare to kick it?*

The deep, kind voice said, "Sí." But David said no. He let the ball roll by him.

One of the Sharks laughed. David was so embarrassed! He hated to play soccer in a real game! He wanted to quit. But he couldn't.

David made himself run down the field.

No one on his team passed him the ball. No one on the other team guarded him. He was such a bad player that everyone ignored him.

A Shark was dribbling the ball. He was the one who had laughed at David. All of a sudden, he tripped and fell down.

The soccer ball rolled to David. "Should I kick it?" he asked himself.

"Sí," said the voice. This time David listened.

"¡Sí!" he shouted. He kicked the ball hard. The ball shot into the goal. Score! The game was now 2 – 1!

Miguel hugged him. The Eagle fans cheered. David felt great!

The Sharks were still winning, however.

The Sharks had the ball at midfield. One of them kicked it high in the air. It was coming down near David.

Should he head it?

"Sí," said the voice.

"¡Sí!" yelled David. He was no longer afraid.

Bam! He headed the ball to Miguel, who was ready for it. With one swift kick, it was in! The score was now 2 − 2.

"¡Bien!" shouted Tío.

David hugged Miguel.

"Abuelito's here! I can feel him!" said Miguel. "We're going to win!"

The Sharks had expected to win easily. Now they were mad. Now they played better than ever.

They ran well. But so did the Eagles.

They headed the ball well. So did the Eagles.

Both goalies made great saves. No one scored.

Only a minute was left in the game. The Eagles took the ball down the field.

David ran as fast as he could. But he couldn't keep up. He was getting tired. He was left behind. No one was covering him.

Miguel took a shot at the goal.

The ball bounced off the goal post. It shot back toward David.

David had no time to ask if he should kick it or not. He just said "¡Sí!" and kicked. The ball sailed over the other players' heads and landed in the goal.

The Eagles won the game and the tournament! David was a hero!

◆

David had never been so happy, but he wished his mother was there, too.

It was David's last night in Mexico.

"Abuelita wants to hear the story again," said Miguel.

They were sitting outside. The air was cool and peaceful.

"During games I used to ask myself, 'Should I?' I always answered 'No,'" said David. "Today I learned to say 'Sí.'"

Abuelita smiled. She said something in Spanish.

"She said that Abuelito was never afraid of anything," said Miguel.

"That's why he was a champion," said David.

"That's why we're champs, too!" said Miguel.

David replayed the game in his mind all the way home. He was sad to leave Mexico, but he couldn't wait to see his mom.

"Prepare for landing," said the pilot.

David's mother was thrilled to see him. She loved her many presents, too. Tía had sent a colorful blouse. Tío had sent a fancy tin mirror. Abuelita had sent silver earrings and a box of homemade chocolates.

The last present was the best. "From me and Abuelito," said David.

David's mother unwrapped the paper. Inside were two medals. The first was the lucky medal of Abuelito's. The second was the medal David had won.

"But what about you?" asked his mother.

"I have a trophy!" cried David. He pulled the beautiful gold trophy out of his suitcase. In small letters it said LAS ÁGUILAS. In big letters it said CHAMPIONS.

The next year David played on a real soccer team again.

He ran. He kicked the ball. He scored! His team was the best in the league.

After the last game, he called Miguel. "Guess what?" he said. "We are going to play in a tournament on November 2. Do you want to come and visit?"

"But I'll miss the Day of the Dead!" said Miguel.

"No, you won't," said David. "I've already started to make the altar!"